COLORING BOOK ABOUT THE SACRAMENTS

Adapted from the Picture Book "The Seven Sacraments"
of Father Lawrence G. Lovasik, S.V.D.
Illustrated by

PAUL T. BIANCA

CATHOLIC BOOK PUBLISHING CO.
NEW YORK

Through the Seven Sacraments, Jesus comes to us and gives us the grace we need to save our souls.

(T-687)

NIHIL OBSTAT: Daniel V. Flynn, J.C.D., *Censor Librorum*
IMPRIMATUR: Patrick J. Sheridan
Vicar General, Archdiocese of New York

BAPTISM

PENANCE

HOLY EUCHARIST

CONFIRMATION

MARRIAGE

ANOINTING OF THE SICK

HOLY ORDERS

The Sacraments are like seven rivers of grace flowing from our Savior on the Cross, through the Catholic Church.

Baptism

Jesus told his Apostles to baptize all people in the Name of the Father, and of the Son, and of the Holy Spirit.

BAPTISM

Baptism incorporates us into Christ. It removes original sin and personal sin, if any. It makes us members of the Church and gives us a right to go to heaven.

PENANCE

Jesus gave His Apostles the power to forgive sins in His Name.

We look at Jesus suffering on the Cross for our sins. We tell Him
we are sorry for our sins and ask for His forgiveness.

PENANCE

We tell our sins to the priest. The priest forgives us in the Name of Jesus.

PENANCE

Through frequent confession Jesus gives us
His own peace and joy.

9

HOLY EUCHARIST

At the Last Supper, Jesus changed bread and wine into His Body and Blood. Then He told His Apostles to do this in memory of Him.

HOLY EUCHARIST

At Mass, the priest does what Jesus did. The bread and wine become the Body and Blood of Jesus.

HOLY EUCHARIST

Holy Mass makes present for us the Passion and Death, Resurrection and Ascension of Jesus.

HOLY EUCHARIST

In the Sacrament of the Eucharist, God gives us the best Gift He has—
His own loving Son, our God and Savior.

HOLY EUCHARIST

On certain days of the year, we honor Jesus in the Blessed Sacrament with a procession around the Church.

HOLY EUCHARIST

We sing hymns and say prayers to Jesus, our Lord and Savior.
He is present in the Sacred Host that is carried by the priest.

CONFIRMATION

After Jesus went to heaven, the Holy Spirit came down on Mary, His Mother, and the Apostles in the form of a dove and tongues of fire.

CONFIRMATION

When we receive Confirmation, the Bishop anoints us on the forehead and prays for the Seven Gifts of the Holy Spirit.

The Holy Spirit gives us His strength and helps us to learn our Catholic religion.

CONFIRMATION

The Holy Spirit helps us to lead good Catholic lives and give good example to others—for example, by taking the blame when we do wrong.

MARRIAGE

Jesus taught that Marriage is a Sacrament that unites a man with a woman and creates a Christian family.

MARRIAGE

In Marriage, the husband and wife give the Sacrament
to one another in the presence of a priest.

MARRIAGE

Marriage helps Mothers and Fathers to love one another and bring children into the world.

MARRIAGE

The Sacrament of Marriage helps all members of the family to live in peace with one another.

HOLY ORDERS

When Jesus had gone to heaven, the Apostles placed their hands on the heads of certain men and made them priests.

HOLY ORDERS

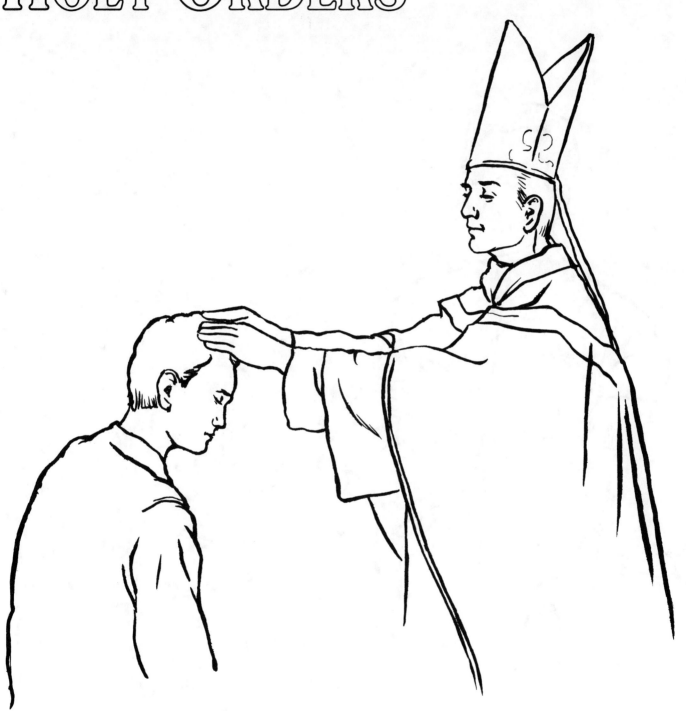

The Sacrament of Holy Orders makes certain men like Jesus and gives them sacred power to serve the People of God.

HOLY ORDERS

Priests teach us about the truth that Jesus came to give all people.

HOLY ORDERS

Priests have the power to make us holy and help us to be worthy to reach heaven.

ANOINTING OF THE SICK

After Jesus went to heaven, the Apostles went about anointing those who were seriously ill, infirm, and aged.

ANOINTING OF THE SICK

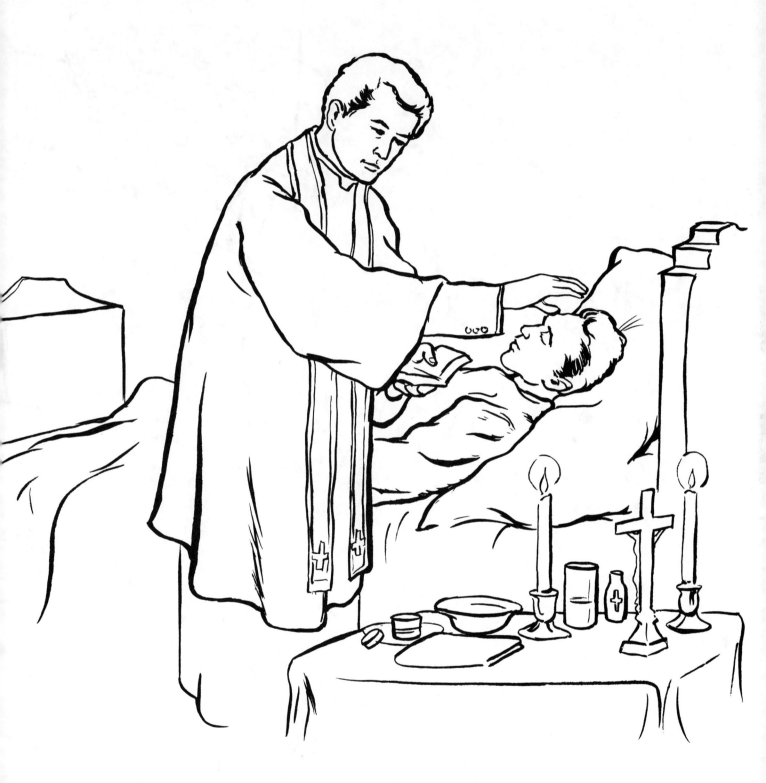

The Sacrament of the Anointing of the Sick is given
to those seriously ill and those who are aged.

ANOINTING OF THE SICK

Sometimes many sick people are anointed together in the church.

ANOINTING OF THE SICK

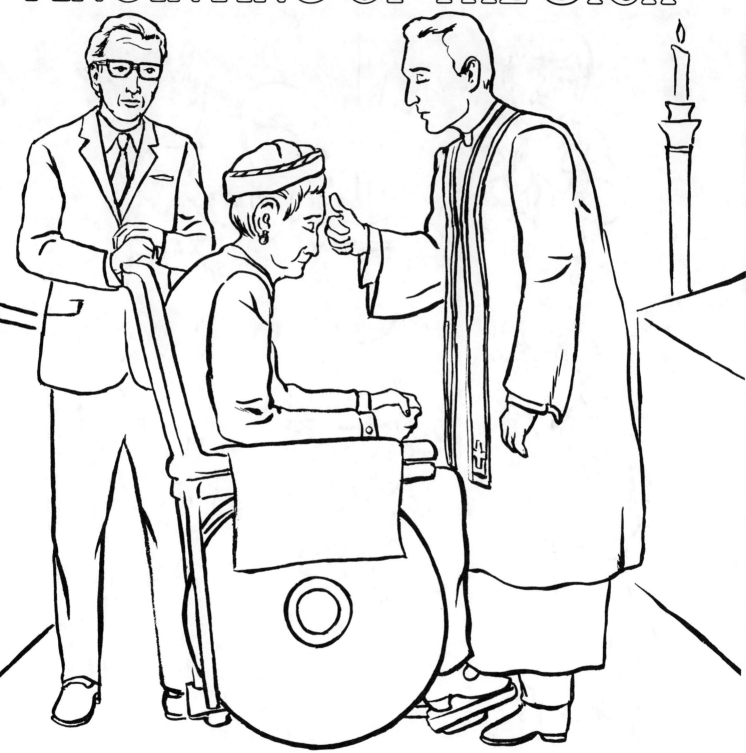

The Sacrament of Anointing helps the sick in their suffering,
forgives their sins, and brings them to salvation.

We thank God for the Sacraments—especially the
Eucharist, which is the greatest Sacrament.